Dolly and the Train

Heather Amery

Illustrated by Stephen Cartwright

Language consultant: Betty Root
Series editor: Jenny Tyler

There is a little yellow duck to find on every page.

This is Apple Tree Farm.

This is Mrs. Boot, the farmer. She has two children,
called Poppy and Sam, and a dog called Rusty.

Today there is a school outing.

Mrs. Boot, Poppy and Sam walk down the road to the old station. "Come on, Rusty," says Sam.

"There's your teacher," says Mrs. Boot.

"And there's the old steam train, all ready for our outing," says Poppy.

"All aboard," says the driver.

The children and their teacher climb on the train.
The guard closes the door and blows his whistle.

Mrs. Boot waves goodbye.

The train puffs slowly down the track. Rusty barks
at it. He wants to go on the outing too.

The children look out of the window.

"I can see Farmer Dray's farm," says Sam.
"Why has the train stopped?" asks Poppy.

"The engine has broken down."

"We'll have to send for help," says the driver.
"It won't be long." The guard runs across the fields.

"Here's a ladder."

"You can all get off now," says the driver. "We can have our picnic here," says the teacher.

"Let's go into the field," says Sam.

The children climb over the fence. "Stop! Come back, children," says the teacher. "There's a bull."

"It's only Buttercup."

"She's not a bull. She's a very nice cow," says Poppy.
"Well, come back here," says the teacher.

"Look, there's Farmer Dray."

"He's brought Dolly with him," says Sam. "A horse is no good. We need an engine," says the teacher.

The children watch.

Farmer Dray has a long rope. He leads Dolly along the train. The driver unhitches the engine.

The children climb back on the train.

"We'll soon be off now," says the teacher.
"Dolly's ready," says Farmer Dray.

"Pull away, Dolly."

Dolly pulls and pulls. Very slowly the train starts to move. Farmer Dray walks along with Dolly.

They reach the station.

"Out by engine, back by horse," says Farmer Dray.
"That was a good outing," says Sam.

Cover design by Hannah Ahmed   Digital manipulation by Nelupa Hussain